GIFT

Billy-William Bigheart

Billy-William Bigheart
The Kindest Boy in the Universe

by
Susan Hill

Illustrated by Helen Lang

Little Barn Books

For Lila
S.H.

For Danielle
H.L.

One

When a bouncing baby boy was born to Mr and Mrs Bigheart, of Number 100, Jubilee Road.

The baby's Mum wanted to call him BILLY.

And his Dad wanted to call him WILLIAM.

So, because they never ever quarrelled they agreed that his Mum would call him BILLY, his Dad would call him WILLIAM and everyone else would call him BILLY-WILLIAM. (Though his best friend Jim Jelly always called him 'BILL'.)

The Bighearts were a delightful and loving family.

Cheerful. Contented. Peaceable. Friendly. Happy. And very hospitable.

Bigheart by name and Bigheart by nature.

But Billy-William was the Bigheart with the biggest heart of all.

As he grew up, he quickly became the Kindest Boy in Jubilee Road.

He helped old ladies across the road.

He carried their heavy shopping bags.

When Mrs McCreedy-at-Number-10's buggy broke down, he pushed it all the way home

WITH MRS McCREEDY IN IT.

He fetched the newspaper every day for Mr O'Shea at Number 14.

He picked up the litter that people had thrown into the front garden of Number 11.

He helped to clear the snow from the footpaths in winter. He helped his Dad scrape the ice off his car windscreen.

He even gave his LAST CHEW BAR to the little girl who lived at Number 60, when she dropped hers in the mud.

Billy-William Bigheart was kind to

Old people

Young people

Small girls

Small boys,

Babies.

But most of all he was kind to

ANIMALS.

He stroked cats.

Patted dogs.

Gave carrots to horses.

Picked groundsel for the chickens at Number 89.

Rescued migrating toads from the middle of the road.

He even made a sign and got his Dad to put it up.

DRIVE SLOWLY. TOADS CROSSING.

Once, he led a mother duck and her eleven ducklings to safety in the pond.

He put out toast and biscuit crumbs for the birds.

And saved mice from being jumped on by
CATS.

He even liked *insects* and was kind to

Spiders

Flies

Ladybirds

Ants

Beetles.

He was also especially kind to WORMS.

If all this makes Billy-William Bigheart sound like a

GOODY-GOODY, A CREEP and a SUCK, Well

He wasn't.

He was often

Naughty Cheeky Silly Rude Messy Forgetful Thoughtless and even

DOWNRIGHT DISOBEDIENT.

He played tricks on teachers,

Hadn't washed behind his ears or brushed his teeth or put on clean socks.

When he said he had.

He lost things all the time.

Pens

Shoelaces

Handkerchiefs

Dinner money

Important notes from school to his Mum
and from his Mum to school.

He ate too many chew bars,

And not enough vegetables.

He even slipped beans and peas and sprouts
and carrots into his pockets.

And gave them to hungry animals he met.

In other words, Billy-William Bigheart was

A perfectly normal boy.

But that didn't stop him from being

The Kindest Boy in Jubilee Road,

And probably in the whole town

And even

THE WHOLE COUNTRY.

Mr and Mrs Bigheart were very proud of their son and his kindness.

Mrs Bigheart never minded when Billy brought people home to tea unexpectedly.

School Friends

Neighbours

An old lady who looked lonely

An old man with a bad leg

People who didn't have homes.

But most of all, his best friend

JIM JELLY,

Who came to tea most days

And quite often to breakfast.

Jim Jelly was a peculiar looking boy

With large ears that stuck out

Hair that stuck up

Long long thin thin arms that dangled

Big feet

And a huge chin.

He led a sad life in many ways.

He had an older brother who picked on him and told tales.

He was beaten up in the school playground because of his ears and his hair and his long long thin thin arms and his big feet and his huge chin.

His mother worked late shifts at a gym so he didn't see her much.

His father worked such long hours in his office to make loads of money

that when he did come home and Jim wanted to talk to him

he was often asleep.

His sister was supposed to get his tea but she usually forgot, because she was getting ready to go out

Or on her phone

Or her laptop, chatting to her friends.

So Jim Jelly came round to the Bigheart's house a lot,

Billy-William's Mum tried to cheer him up with

Chicken curry and rice

Treacle sponge and custard

Roast beef and Yorkshire pudding

Roast Lamb and mint sauce

Sausages and mash

Cheese on toast

Eggs and bacon

Pancakes and sugar

Apple crumble
Steak pie and peas
Chocolate fudge cake
Flapjacks
Stockpot soup
Porridge with sugar and cream.

Jim Jelly ate all these in huge quantities.
He ate more than Mr Bigheart, but even so
he stayed thin

And sad.

His saddest times were

Christmas and his birthday.

Because, when Billy-William Bigheart
and other boys got games and bikes and
footballs and sweets

Jim got

CLOTHES.

Socks

School shirts

Pants

Vests

Woolly hats

Warm gloves

Pyjamas.

Jumpers

Though once, as a special treat, he did get

A NEW PENCIL CASE.

If Mr and Mrs Jelly had been very poor this
might have been quite understandable.

But they had loads of money

They just didn't see the point in wasting it
on toys and games.

Poor Jim.

Billy-William was very kind to his best friend
and so were Mr and Mrs Bigheart.

Jim was welcome at their house any time

For Breakfast, Elevenses, Lunch, Tea, Supper

And in between.

He absolutely loved going to the Bigheart's,

Because there was always something mad
going on –

LIKE

Mr Bigheart practising golf in the living
room

even though he didn't actually play the game

Mrs Bigheart dying her own hair, sometimes
pink or with purple streaks.

Everyone playing Sardines or Pin the Tail on the Donkey just because they felt like having some fun.

Or wearing paper hats left over from Christmas

Or suddenly deciding to go for fish and chips

And eat them out of the paper, sitting on a wall.

At the Jelly's house the food was very boring.

It was fat free

Sugar free

Dairy free

Artificial colouring free

Salt free

And there was an awful lot of

Salad

Brown food like beans and lentils and nut roast

And more salad

And salad again.

They never had sponge puddings or pancakes or ice cream or jelly or trifle or cakes or biscuits or chocolate or jam

EVER

Billy-William Bigheart

You can see why Jim was so often at the Bigheart's house.

One Saturday, Billy-William had been watering the plants and flowers for Mrs Sparks, the old lady at Number 84.

First he did the flower beds, then the pots and tubs and hanging baskets.

It took AGES.

'Billy-William Big-heart, you are the kindest boy I ever knew,' the old lady said, when the watering was finished at last.

And she opened her sweet tin, as she always did, and offered it to him.

'Take two,' she said.

So he took two. As he always did. It had been a long time since breakfast and he couldn't wait to gobble up his huge lemon and raspberry fruit drop but he put the second one in his pocket, to give to Jim Jelly when they met up.

Which was about ten seconds later because Jim was waiting for him at the gate.

They mooched along sucking their fruit drops, wondering what the day would bring.

At various times, the day had brought

A mega snowstorm

A military band on parade

A police car racing past them, with blue light whirling and siren wailing. It had stopped a bit further up the road. Four cops had got out and gone charging up an alleyway.

Once, a girl had fallen off her bike right beside them, and hurt her arm badly. Billy-William had run to a house for help, Jim had stayed to comfort her and when the ambulance had arrived, they had both been congratulated.

Mostly, nothing much happened but they enjoyed mooching along all the same and if it rained they went back to Billy-William's house and played what Jim's parents called 'Time-wasting games.'

In his house there were only had Educational and Instructive and Improving games.

So they didn't go there when it rained.

Today

Nothing had happened so far. Nothing at all.

But ...

EVERYTHING WAS ABOUT TO CHANGE!

They had mooched down the road in the sunshine, kicking a stone between them, and turned the corner leading to the shops.

At first, everything seemed to be the same as usual.

But then, Jim Jelly pointed.

'That wasn't there before,' he said.

'That's the shop that sells nails and screws and electric plugs and mops ...'

'And brooms and floor polish and dusters.'

'And paint.'

'Only it doesn't now.'

The sign above the shop used to say

BRUSH AND BUCKET

IRONMONGER HARDWARE
LOCKSMITH
EVERYTHING FOR THE HANDYMAN

It had been dark inside and had smelled
of paraffin, with old-fashioned floorboards
covered in wood shavings.

Billy-William and Jim Jelly had been in
occasionally, on errands to buy a light bulb
or a battery for someone.

They had got what they needed, then
scuttled out again, watched closely by

Mr Brush or Mr Bucket, who did not care for SMALL BOYS.

'It's not as if we wanted to pinch a feather duster,' Billy-William had said.

'Or a tin of varnish.'

But Broom and Bucket had vanished.

Now the sign over the shop said

SPAVIN AND LAME

PETS and PET SUPPLIES

The boys went over and peered in the window.

There was very little to see inside the shop.

A sack of dog biscuits

A bale of hay

A tin of

POWDER TO KILL CA ...

They couldn't read the rest because the tin
was turned away from them, but it didn't
sound good.

There was a metal basket with a few squeaky
toys in the bottom and a cardboard label

EVERYTHING HERE.
50P TO CLEAR

'It says 'PETS' 'Jim Jelly said. 'Only I can't see any.'

'They must be getting everything ready. Next time we come it will be full of them.'

'What sort of Pets?'

'The usual sort. Rabbits. Guinea pigs. Hamsters. Budgies.'

'Snakes. I always wanted a pet snake.'

'Your Mum wouldn't let you. She wouldn't even let you have a pet flea.'

'*Especially* not a pet flea.'

Billy-William saw the sad and lonely expression on his friend's face. It came sometimes, like a cloud across the sun.

'Come on, I just found 20 pence in my pocket. That's four chew bars – two each.'

On the way home Billy-William was thoughtful. Then he said, in between chews, 'There was something funny about that pet shop.'

Jim Jelly couldn't answer because he had taken a MASSIVE bite of his chew and it had stuck his teeth together.

'The sign wasn't a proper sign like the old one. That was painted on wood and varnished. This one was just black paint on an old plank, nailed up. The letters weren't even the same size.'

Jim swallowed.

'And why weren't there any pets?'

'I expect they were in the back where we couldn't see. I expect they'll be opening properly soon.'

'So you don't think there was anything funny after all? I wish you'd make up your mind.'

They had reached Billy-William's gate. His Mum was at the front door.'

'There you are. You look as if you've had a fun morning.'

Jim Jelly sighed, his Mum would have said he looked as if he'd been 'up to something' and told him off for getting his clothes dirty or his shoes muddy.

Or both.

'Meat and potato pie and baked apples for lunch. I daresay you're stopping, Jim.'

'Yes PLEASE!'

He and Billy-William did a hi-five and raced into the house.

SPAVIN AND LAME

PETS PET SUPPLIES

Was forgotten.

For the time being.

Two

What with one thing and another, the two boys didn't get back to the shops for a whole week and a day.

The 'things' included

Haircuts

Dentist

Buying new shoes

Visiting Aunties and Uncles

And for Jim Jelly

Five days at his Granny's, while his parents were at a Health Farm.

It was awful. His Granny was his Mum's mother. They were very alike, especially in their worst aspects.

They were both fussy and their food was terrible.

Possibly it was even worse at his Gran's than at home, because she hated cooking, so they ate raw salads a lot – salads full of red cabbage and white cabbage and grated carrots and red onion and nuts and seeds that stuck in the gaps between your teeth.

There were only two things to drink.

Water. Which was OK – boring, but OK.

And milk made out of coconuts, which was so disgusting that once Jim had tried it, he felt ill for an entire day. After that he stuck to water.

There was no one to mooch about with and no visits to the Bighearts to get delicious food.

It was a very very bad week and Jim Jelly was

SUNKEN IN GLOOM.

But it did come to an end at last and the day after he got back, Jim met Billy-William on the corner.

'Last week of the holidays.' Jim Jelly said.

'Got to make the most of it.'

'I've got 20p.'

'Chew Bars!'

They raced off down the road. But when they came to the shops, they stopped dead.

SPAVIN AND LAME.

PETS. PET SUPPLIES.

MEGA CLOSING DOWN SALE.

EVERYTHING MUST GO.

NO SENSIBLE OFFER REFUSED.

LAST CHANCE TO GET YOURSELF AN
UNUSUAL PET.

CROCODILE – 2NDS. (NO TEETH).
GOING CHEAP.

CAMEL. (LAST ONE) NO HUMP.
(ALMOST) FREE TO GOOD HOME.

They read the notices and then read them
again, out loud.

'That's queer. They only opened last week.'

'Business must have been bad.'

'Oh noooooo! Look ...'

Underneath all the other notices was one in
smaller letters.

'Shutting Friday. All pets remaining unsold will be DISPOSED OF.'

The boys looked at one another in horror.

'WHAT?'

'WHAT?'

Jim Jelly peered in through one shop window, and Billy-William peered through the other.

But then they both leaped into the air as someone peered back.

The next minute, the shop door had opened and a man came out.

He was small and incredibly thin and incredibly bald – except for a few tufts of hair on top of his head.

He had an incredibly big nose.

And an unpleasant expression.

'Why, hello, dear boys! How good to see you. So, you've noticed the signs.

DO come in.'

He crooked a long dirty finger and smiled with long yellow and brown teeth, which were shaped like tombstones.

'Come in, come in ...'

He held the door open. The boys looked into

the darkness at the back of the shop. It was like a cave.

'You like pets, I know you do ... and there's a pet for every occasion. You're sure to find something to love.'

Before they could stop him, the man had reached out a long thin arm and grabbed first Billy-William, then Jim Jelly and pulled them inside the shop. Then, quick as a flash, he had locked the door and swivelled the sign round from OPEN to CLOSED.

They still couldn't see much, apart from the bale of hay and the dog biscuits. Jim Jelly noticed that the tin with POWDER FOR KILLING CA ...' had gone from the shelf. The basket of squeaky toys 'All at 50p to clear' was still there.

'I'm sorry but we should be going,' Jim said, his voice sounding weird and quavery. 'We ... We have to be ... erm ... we have to get home.'

'That's right,' Billy-William said, turning to the door. 'Thank you all the same, we'd love to see the pets – another day.'

But as he put his hand to the door catch, the man's arm shot out and grabbed his in a nasty grip. His long fingers seemed to have turned into claws which held onto Billy-William's arm tightly.

'No, no, you're definitely going to see the PETS. Now, come this way ... through to the back. Some of them are here and a lot are in the garden and the conservatory and ...' All the time he was talking he was grinning with his

nasty teeth and all the time he was talking and grinning, he was pulling them further and further into the dark depths at the back of the shop. He had a hand on each of them and his grip was like a pair of pliers digging into their arms.

The back room was lit by one dim bulb hanging from the ceiling. Leading off it was another room and beyond that they could see a yard and a long strip of brownish grass.

There were dilapidated old sheds and a
wooden stable that looked as if they might
collapse at any moment.

'Come along, dear boys, come and see ...
something to tempt you, something you
will be delighted to take home? Because of
course, if you don't, I'm sad to say ...'

The back room smelled of dirty straw and
animal poo and horse hair and damp fur.

There were a lot of cages, piled on top of each other. Eyes gleamed out of them from every one – yellow eyes, green eyes, orange eyes, dark brown eyes. Red eyes.

Billy-William reached out and grabbed Jim Jelly's arm.

'This is horrible!' he whispered.

'It's worse than that,' Jim said.

'All going cheap … cheaper than cheap … come and look …'

The man was trying to get hold of them again but this time, Billy-William had stepped back.

'How much is 'cheap'?'

The man's eyes flashed and a greedy look came over his face.

'VERY Cheap … everything must go …'

'It's no use saying 'cheap' – tell us HOW MUCH?'

The man rubbed his hands together, which made a dry, scratchy sound.

'It all depends on what you want to take home, my dear. These lovely sweet-faced little rats, now, Buy One Get One Free.'

'What does one cost?'

'er ... five pounds.'

'I haven't got five pounds.'

'I mean one pound, of course ...'

'I don't even have ...'

'That's fifty pence each, plus free rat food ...'

'I'll have to think about it.'

'Or a camel? There's a handsome camel outside, straight from the perfumed deserts of Arabia ... cheap to feed, very reliable. A camel makes a loving pet.'

'I don't think ...'

Quick as lightening, the man grabbed Jim Jelly. 'Or ...' he said, leaning towards Jim and breathing into his face, 'OR, a ssssssnake ...'

'My Mum ...'

'Lovely surprise for Mother's Day, quite right.'

'My Mum ...'

'Mother's Day is in March,' Billy-Wiliam said, 'and this is the end of August. Now, let him go please.'

'All these pets will be gone by tomorrow night, and when I say 'gone' I mean

G.O.N.E. GONE ...'

Three

After they had escaped from the clutches
of the pet shop man, Billy-William and Jim
Jelly had mooched home in gloomy silence.
Even the freshly baked sausage rolls and
flapjacks in Mrs Bigheart's kitchen didn't
really cheer them up, though they ate four
each, to see if they would.

'What's come over the two of you, with faces
like a wet Wednesday?' Mrs Bigheart asked,
pouring them a second glass of cherryade.

'Nothing.'

'Nothing.'

'Well if that's the truth, you can take your
miseries in the other room and watch a film,
or go outside and play in the garden. I don't
want to catch whatever it is you've got.'

They went outside and sat on the wall, not saying anything.

Just looking.

The garden at the Bigheart's house was long and at the end of it was a fence. On the other side of the fence was a field. Sometimes there were cows in the field, once there had been three horses, and a year or so ago there had been sheep. But now, there was nothing but grass and weeds and a couple of old sheds. Mr Bigheart occasionally talked about keeping chickens. Or pigs. But nothing ever came of it.

Jim Jelly sighed. 'I have to be home by four o'clock.'

'What for?'

'My Aunty and my Gran are coming for tea.'

'Bad luck.' Jim Jelly's Aunty was all right, if you didn't mind the very strong smell of moth balls and peppermint, because that's what she always smelled of, but his Granny was a nightmare, a sour faced, whiskery-chinned, sniffy nosed, runny-eyed, crotchety, cranky, miserable, mean woman who had never said one single kind word to Jim since he was born.

'I have to be there.'

'I know.'

'See you.'

'See you.'

Jim mooched slowly off up the road, dragging his feet in the dust. Billy-William felt sorry for him but there was nothing he could do to help – except go into the kitchen, load some flapjacks and sausage rolls and a slice of ginger cake on a plate and put them in the pantry, for Jim to eat when he came round the next day.

That night he couldn't sleep. He lay awake looking at the sky through a chink in the curtains.

He got up and went for a wee.

He came back to bed and lay awake some more, looking at the football poster on his wall.

He got up and had a drink of water.

The clock ticked round ...

Round ...

Round ...

Until it reached

FIVE PAST TWO

And Billy-William Bigheart still wasn't
asleep.

He was worrying.

He kept thinking about the horrible pet shop
man.

The sad animals.

The sign that said

'EVERYTHING MUST GO.'

The worry was going round in his mind like
a hundred hamsters on their wheels ...

But then he sat up SUDDENLY.

The solution had gone POP! inside his brain.

He knew exactly what he could do and
should do and absolutely

WAS GOING TO DO.

He was so pleased and so excited that he almost rushed into his Mum and Dad's bedroom to tell them.

But he stopped himself just in time.

The only thing he wasn't sure about was, when?

He wanted to do it now but that was a really stupid idea.

He couldn't manage by himself.

It was the middle of the night.

He only had to wait until after breakfast,
when he could put his plan into action.

He turned his head on his pillow one more
time.

A millionth of a second later

He was fast tight deeply totally absolutely
completely

ASLEEP.

Four

The second his eyes opened the next morning he remembered everything and his tummy gave a big lurch.

He put his t-shirt on back to front, which didn't matter much, and his pants as well which would cause problems later, and he forgot to put socks on before his shoes. He was in such a rush to get downstairs that he forgot to do up his shoe laces. With

DISASTROUS RESULTS.

When Mrs Bigheart had picked him up and put a sticking plaster on his knee, Billy-William ate a bowl of porridge with brown sugar and cream, grabbed a banana from the dish and hurtled out through the back door.

'William Bigheart, COME BACK HERE!'

His Dad was frowning.

'Put your bowl and spoon in the sink, go upstairs and brush your teeth and say 'Thank You' nicely to your mum for your breakfast.'

'Thank you nicely, Mum.'

Billy-William shot up the stairs, rubbed a brush hastily over his front teeth and shot down again.

'AND?'

'And please may I go out now?'

Mrs Bigheart looked at her only son. He was a mess. A COMPLETE AND TOTAL MESS.

She sighed. When was he ever NOT a mess, unless it was a school day and she had made sure he was wearing clean pants and vest, a freshly ironed shirt, shoes AND socks, and that he had brushed his hair and teeth and ...?

She started laughing. 'Billy Bigheart, you'll be the death of me. Go on, out with you, and don't get into any trouble and if you want to bring Jim Jelly back for dinner ...'

But he was already half way down the front path and couldn't hear a word his mother said.

He knew that Jim Jelly wouldn't be around and at the back of his mind was still the worry that he probably couldn't do this alone. But as there was no time to be lost, and every second counted, he would just have to find a way.

He raced down the road and turned the corner.

PHEW!

It was still there. Things had been happening in such a peculiar way lately that he been afraid the pet shop might have vanished into thin air overnight, or that it would be completely empty, with a TO LET sign over the door.

'Hello, my dear. I had a feeling that you'd be back!'

The nasty pet shop man reached out to grab him by the arm but Billy-William dodged.

'So – have you come to choose a pet? Everything's still here ... the crocodile with no teeth would suit you very nicely ... or the straight snake. Did you see the straight snake? It is of course extremely rare. Most snakes can coil themselves round – but not this one. Or maybe you'd rather just have a cage full of white rats ... there were two yesterday but, lo and behold, this morning there are ELEVEN. Dear little things! But you want to take a look around again, I'm sure … come to a proper decision after careful thought? Quite right. I could see you were a thoughtful boy the moment you came in through that door.'

He grinned a horrible grin.

There was no one else in the shop and when he looked out of the window Billy-William saw that the street was empty too. He felt extremely nervous, alone in the dingy, dim pet shop with scrabbling scratching sounds coming from cages all round and yellow, green and red eyes peering at him.

He knew what he wanted to say and he knew what he wanted to do. But for some odd reason the words wouldn't come out of his mouth. He looked round. The pet shop man looked round. They looked at each other.

And then, the door opened and into the shop came Jim Jelly.

Billy-William had never been so pleased to see anyone in his entire life.

'But ... but I thought you ...'

'It's OK,' Jim said, 'My Granny's got a bad cold. They're not coming.'

The boys did a high-five as the pet shop man stood looking sour, and grinding his yellow teeth.

'Now look here, no packs of kids in my shop, crowding the place out, causing trouble. One at a time is my rule so YOU ...' he pointed a long yellow fingernail on the end of a long thin yellow finger, at Jim Jelly.

'OUT!'

'He's come to help me,' Billy-William said, 'I'll need it.'

'Have I? Will you?' Jim looked puzzled.

'I have decided,' Billy-William said. 'Actually, I'd decided before I even came into the shop.

I'd decided when I was here yesterday.'

'I like a little boy who knows his mind,' the pet shop man said, grinning horribly again now and rubbing his hands dryly together with a noise like scratchy paper.

'What dear little creature is it to be? A white mouse or three? Or perhaps that little singing canary hanging in its cage up there? Such a sweet song ...'

The totally silent canary sat looking depressed and dull on its perch.

'I am going to buy ...'

Jim Jelly looked worried. He was afraid that his friend would choose something unsuitable, like a donkey, and he wasn't sure how Mrs Bigheart would react. True, he had never ever known her to be anything but sunny and cheerful, or ever heard her shout or grumble. All the same, most mothers would be entitled to complain if a donkey came in through the back door.

Billy-William Bigheart held out his hand. It contained a fifty pence piece, a ten pence piece and a few pennies.

'Whatever I can have for this much ...' he said.

The pet shop man gave a nasty laugh. 'Perhaps ... a FLEA?' he said.

'AND ...' Billy-William pointed in turn to a cage of white mice, a cage of hamsters, a cage of gerbils, a budgerigar, two canaries and a parrot.

'And all those. And I would like you to deliver them please. My address is Number 100, Jubilee Road. The name is Bigheart.'

Jim Jelly went white. He tried to attract his friend's attention but Billy-William wasn't looking.

He nudged him urgently. 'Bill ...'

'In a minute.'

'But your Mum ...'

'I said, in a MINUTE.' He turned back to the pet shop man. 'Here is the money. You said 'Everything must go,' right?'

The pet shop man had begun to look suspicious. He sucked in his cheeks and wiped his hand over his mouth. 'Weeeeelllll ...'

'Right?'

There was a pause. The man was thinking furiously, you could tell that by the way his eyes had sunk back into his head and were crossed, so that he could focus better.

Jim Jelly daren't say anything else, he just stood and worried. He was very fond of his friend Bill and he didn't want him to get into terrible trouble, as a result of being kind. It had happened quite a few times before.

'All righteeeee,' the pet shop man said now, grinning a yellow grin. 'You're quite correct in what you say. Everything must go. In fact, I've got the lorries booked now to take them all to the ...'

'We don't want to hear, thanks, we can guess. So, you've got the money. If you could bring the things I asked for and ... and anything else you can add in extra ... 100 Jubilee Road. Any time today. Goodbye ...'

And he marched to the shop door. Jim Jelly followed, trying to make himself small, his face scrumpled up with worry.

When they got to the corner, he said, 'Listen ...'

'Oh don't look like that, it'll be fine. He'll just bring the white mice. He's in it for the money, you can see ... and I only gave him sixty eight pence. He won't even throw in the cage for that, I'll have to get Dad to look in his shed ... there's always a wooden crate or something. Come on.'

He went ahead, whistling cheerfully. He was so full of the joys of the morning and so pleased with himself about what he had just done, that Jim Jelly hadn't the heart to say 'But ...' again. He just caught up and walked beside him, up Jubilee Road.

But he still couldn't stop worrying.

Lunch was fish and chips and strawberry flan and ice cream and Jim Jelly could hardly eat anything.

Mrs Bigheart looked at him hard. 'Are you sickening for something?'

'I dddddd don't thhhhink so.'

'Is there something wrong with my cooking?'

'No ... it's great. It's always great. I'm sorry, Mrs Bigheart.'

'You don't have to be sorry, Jim, but if you feel sick or you've got a pain or ...'

'Well ...' Jim saw that Billy-William was looking at him across the table in a dark way.

'I might be feeling a little bit sick ...'

'Hm. Maybe you should lie down on the sofa in the front room. I'll bring you a glass of water and put a quilt over you. Maybe you'd better have a plastic bowl as well, just in case.'

'Thhhh thank yyyyyou ...'

Jim couldn't look across at Bill as he trailed slowly out of the kitchen, with Mrs Bigheart's arm round him comfortingly.

He sipped the water and lay down and had the quilt put over him. Mrs Bigheart closed the door.

It was very very quiet.

He hadn't felt sick really, only worried
and he wasn't sleepy at all, but strangely,
lying there on the big deep soft sofa with a
cushion behind his head, he was so comfy
and peaceful that his eyes did begin to close.

And open again.

And close.

And open again.

And clooose

Zzzzzzzzzzzzzzzzzzzzzzzzzzzzzzzzzzzzzzzzzzzzzz
zzzzzzzzzzzzzz

'Do you think I should ring his Mum?' Mrs Bigheart asked. 'She'll want to know if he isn't well.'

'No she won't, she never wants to know anything about him.'

Sadly, Mrs Bigheart thought, that was true. She found it hard to understand how a mother could be as Mrs Jelly was, but she said,

'I expect she's a good Mum in her own way.'

'No she's not'

'It's just a different way. Maybe I should ring her.'

'He's OK here isn't he? You don't mind him being on our sofa.'

'Of course I don't ... just pop in and see if he wants anything, Billy.'

'He's welcome to come and live here if he wants,' Mr Bigheart said. He had put his paper down. 'Do as your Mum says, William.'

Billy-William went quietly into the front room, and whispered, 'Jim? You OK?'

Silence.

He crept further in and looked at his friend, fast asleep on the sofa. Maybe he was feeling sick. He did look a bit white. Sort of greenish-white.

For a moment, he stood there, wondering what to do. But just as he was wondering, he heard a noise. He went to the window.

A large lorry had stopped outside the house. Behind the lorry, was a removal van and behind the removal van was a pick-up truck and behind the pick-up truck was another and behind that ...

Billy-William whistled. 'Oh nooooo!'

'What?' Jim Jelly sat up looking confused. 'What? What's happening? Why am I ...'

'Never mind. They've arrived and I think there might be more than a few white mice.

QUICK!'

Billy-William shot out of the house just as the nasty pet shop man was opening the back gate of the lorry. He gave a dirty yellow-brown-toothed grin.

'Afternoon,' he said. 'Nice afternoon. Come out fine again.'

He was looking past Billy-William, and Jim Jelly, who was standing close behind him and looking a bit wobbly.

On the front doorstep stood Mrs Bigheart. Behind her stood Mr Bigheart.

'What's all this? Who are you? What's going on?'

There was a lot of noise coming from the lorry, as the pet shop man started to let down the ramp. There was a lot of noise coming from the furniture removal van, the horse box, the pick-up truck and ...

and from the three more HUGE lorries which had pulled up.

'Oh nooooo.'

'BILLY!!!'

'WILLIAM!!!'

'Listen, Mum, you won't mind when you know all about it … honestly you won't … only, they had this sign, it said, EVERYTHING MUST GO OR … and it was awful, they …'

But nobody was listening. They were all too busy staring at what was coming down the front path.

'Where do you want this?' the pet shop man asked. He was leading a camel by an old bit of rope.

'Erm … er … oh, dear … round the back … in the garden?' Mrs Bigheart looked as if she might be going to faint. Jim Jelly was sitting on the step with his head between his knees.

The camel was followed by ...

A donkey

A pig

Two chimpanzees

A cart horse

A cow with one horn

Four geese

Two sheep

A Llama

A long narrow box containing the straight snake

A cage with a large number of white mice

Five rats

A bin labelled BREAD which contained the gerbils

Two budgerigars and four canaries

Three parrots

Two huge fish tanks ... full of fish

And the toothless crocodile in an old sink.

They went in procession down the side path and into the garden, which soon filled up.

So did most of the field behind it.

The fish went into the pond.

The mice and the gerbils, the budgerigars, the canaries and the rats all came into the kitchen.

The toothless crocodile went into the bath.
'Just for now,' Mrs Bigheart said weakly.
'While we think what to do.'

'Do you think I should give him a tip for
bringing them?' Mr Bigheart asked, trying to
laugh but not succeeding very well.

'Right, that's the last armadillo,' the pet shop man said, smirking his nasty smirk. 'And I hope you get a lot of fun and enjoyment out of your new pets. Now, shall we say, two hundred and fifty pounds and a hundred for delivery? And you have a bargain, a fantastic, amazing, BARGAIN.'

'And *you* have to be joking,' Mr Bigheart said, stepping forward accidentally on the man's toe. HARD.

'I'm not giving you a farthing. You're lucky we haven't called the police, dumping all your pets on us to get you out of trouble.'

The pet shop man's face had gone purple with pain and he was hopping about holding his big toe. But when he heard the words 'police ...' and 'trouble ...' and saw that Mr Bigheart's own face was like A

THUNDERCLOUD

He ran. Fast.

Minutes later, all the lorries and vans and pick-ups had gone.

Jubilee Road was empty.

And quiet.

But at the back of the Bigheart's house, it was

VERY NOISY INDEED.

There was

NEIGHING

HISSING

ROARING

HOWLING

BARKING

CHATTERING

MEWING

SQUEALING

GRUNTING

In the kitchen there was

SQUEAKING

And from the bathroom came a gentle

PLOP every now and again, as the toothless
crocodile turned over.

Jim Jelly was hiding behind Billy-William
Bigheart who was hiding behind the hedge.

'Billy!!'
'William!!!!'

He came out very slowly. 'You'll love them.
Honestly. Once you get to know them.
They're all very tame and ... and friendly and

… erm … loveable. And they don't smell or … anything like that, and they don't eat much. Hardly anything at all. And … and they were going to be DISPOSED OF. You couldn't let that happen, could you? You know you couldn't.'

Jim Jelly was shaking so much he made the hedge shake as well. He daredn't even think of what was going to happen to them both, and as for thinking about what his own parents would say when they were told …

The hedge shook so much that it rattled.

Mr and Mrs Bigheart stood side by side, looking at the boys and trying not to pay attention to the racket from behind the house.

'Dad? What did you mean about the police? And 'trouble'?'

After a few seconds, a very small smile crept into the corners of Mr Bigheart's mouth. He tried furiously to hide it but it kept creeping back again.

'Wait there,' he said.

The hedge shook violently again.

'You'd better come out, Jim dear,' Mrs Bigheart said. 'You're doing our hedge no good at all.'

Very very slowly, Jim edged his way out.

'And don't look like that, your face is enough to turn the milk sour.'

Mr Bigheart came out of the house, carrying a newspaper. He opened it. 'Read THIS.'

ZOO BURGLED. DOZENS OF VALUABLE ANIMALS STOLEN.

Beneath the headline was a picture of the pet shop man, looking nasty.

HAVE YOU SEEN THIS MAN?

'That's him! That's him!' Jim shouted.

'POLICE SEEK BOGUS PET SHOP OWNER.'

Police were today looking urgently for Reginald Crook (61) in connection with the theft of a number of exotic animals from a Rescue Zoo. Most of the animals were old, unwell or damaged and were being cared for by the Zoo.

Crook and two other men had been spotted several times at the zoo on previous days and were twice stopped from trying to open a cage and from entering the snake house.

The thieves struck at dead of night and took away a large number of animals, including a toothless crocodile, a straight snake and a one-armed chimpanzee. It is thought that they used a fleet of stolen vehicles.

'This was a wicked burglary of innocent animals,' Mrs Bertha Barnicoot, the Zoo owner said. 'I am in bits, worrying about where they are and what is happening to them. I haven't slept a wink for nights and I can't stop crying.'

Inspector Winston Wellbeloved of the County
Police Force, said, 'This man is known to us from
past criminal activity. He will try to sell these
animals on for profit to unsuspecting members of
the public. If you are offered a toothless crocodile,
a straight snake or any other exotic pet, please
telephone us IMMEDIATELY. Do not attempt to
arrest Reginald Crook, who is known to carry a

tobacco tin containing
a poisonous Black
Widow spider, which
it is feared he may
release at any moment,
with intent to harm.'

'Gosh!'

'Help!'

'Oh noooooo.'

'Right. Now, Dad, while
you phone the police,
I'd better find some
food for these poor
animals ... they're
only making
that racket
because they're
starving.
BOYS!'

Mrs Bigheart managed to find a sack of apples, two bags of peanuts, and three Jumbo Economy sized boxes of porridge oats, as well as carrots and crackers, and the animals were fed. Only the chimpanzee was crying, real tears, because it didn't see anything it liked to eat.

'Billy, go and fetch the bananas from the fruit bowl. Quick! The poor thing's faint with hunger.'

Once they had eaten and drunk about ten gallons of water each and then peed about nine of them out again, the animals settled down and were quiet at last. They looked around them for a while but they were so exhausted with all their comings and goings that most of them went straight to sleep.

Only the hamsters were busy going round on their wheels in the kitchen.

Gradually, everything grew still and peaceful.

'Now then, time I got us something to eat. Are you staying, Jim Jelly? You're very welcome.'

'I don't feel very hungry, Mrs Bigheart.'

'You're not still sick? I'd forgotten all about you in the excitement, poor boy. Do you think you could manage some banana custard? Or a bowl of cornflakes maybe?'

'I could eat a bit of toast. Maybe. I'm not quite sure.'

'I don't wonder ... if your stomach was upset before, it can't have helped having all that panic and palaver. Right, you boys go and watch TV and I'll call you when it's ready. And then it's early bed for you both.'

There wasn't much on TV that they wanted to watch. Billy-William whizzed through the channels and found a re-run of *Dr Doolittle*, who was singing 'Talk to the Animals.'

'I can't face that.'

'Nor me.'

'Is there a Vampire film?'

There was.

In the kitchen, Mrs Bigheart was putting jacket potatoes into the oven and pricking a huge dish of sausages.

'We'll never eat that many.'

'It's those animals I'm thinking of. They'll need breakfast.'

'We can't feed them all for days on end, dear, it's going to be too expensive. Besides, an emergency is one thing but we don't really know what we should be feeding them on, they all have different diets. We could be doing them harm. The best thing will be for me to phone the police and the police will phone the zoo and the zoo will come and fetch them.'

'Not tonight they won't. And you'd better get the garden hose going to fill up all those buckets. I've never seen so much water drunk.'

'Or so much ...'

'George! ... You go and ring that police station. Tea won't be ready for half an hour. I wonder if banana custard is the best thing if Jim's tummy is still upset.'

The police were round in less than a second. Three cars came screaming down Jubilee Road with sirens wailing and blue lights turning.

The lights made Jim Jelly feel poorly again.

But only for a minute. It was actually VERY exciting.

Mrs Bigheart made them all tea and the policemen sat at the kitchen table while they talked to Billy-William and Jim and asked them loads of questions and wrote down loads of notes and drank their tea and ate

AN ENTIRE PLATE OF MRS BIGHEART'S ICED BUNS.

Meanwhile, several neighbours who had complained about the noise the animals were making, now came round to see if they could be of any help.

One man said he was sure he recognised the photo of Reginald Crook.

'I was at school with him fifty years ago,' said another.

And the lady from number 50 said 'I knew that man's mother. Or someone ever so like her.'

And they all told the police what a kind boy Billy-William Bigheart was.

'I'm not a bit surprised he rescued all those animals,' the man from number 44 said.

'He'd do anything for anybody.'

'And we don't mind the noise.'

'Well, not much'

'Hardly at all.'

'Only a tiny bit.'

They all stayed and drank tea too, and another plate of iced buns disappeared.

When everyone had gone, Mrs Bigheart started on their own supper but she looked so exhausted that Mr Bigheart sent her into the front room with a magazine while he took over the cooking.

Billy Bigheart and Jim Jelly laid the table.

In the middle of supper the phone rang. It was the zoo, to say thank you, and that they would be picking their animals up tomorrow.

'Hang on ...' Mr Bigheart said, 'We need to know what the toothless crocodile likes to eat. It's snapping a bit, in a soft, gummy sort of way so I reckon it's hungry.'

He listened carefully.

'It eats …' he said, 'it eats …'

'WHAT?'

Mrs Bigheart and the boys looked at him with their mouths open.

'WHAT?'

So, after supper, Billy-William and his Dad and Jim made a cauldron full, and took it up to the bathroom.

The toothless crocodile was churning the water about in the bath, lashing its tail, and snapping its gummy jaws together.

When it saw what they had brought, it turned over and over, laughing and laughing, and showing all its gums, and thrashing its tail madly.

Carefully, ladle by ladle, Mr Bigheart, Billy-William and Jim slid over the side of the bath into the water – TWO GALLONS OF BANANA CUSTARD.

Five

WHAT HAPPENED IN THE END

Reginald Crook did not go to prison. The Judge said that it was much more important that he find a way of making up for the harm he had done, so he sent him to work for a whole year, without any wages, at the very zoo from which he had stolen the animals.

The zoo people taught him how to look after them all, and he fed and watered them twice a day. He had to

Fill buckets of water

Carry around sacks of
food

Wash the animals down
with hoses

And make huge vats of
banana custard

For the toothless
crocodile.

He even invented a
game.

He coiled up the
straight snake into a tight ring.

Then let him go again

PING

The snake whizzed round very fast until it was straight again.

It loved this game and made Reginald play it with him

OVER AND OVER AND OVER AGAIN.

By the end of the year Reginald had become very fond of all the zoo animals and an expert at looking after them, so the zoo decided to give him a paid job as one of the keepers.

So far as I know

He is still there.

Billy-William Bigheart continued to be such a kind boy that after he had rescued a toddler from being lifted up and carried away by a swan in the park, had stood in front of an old lady's motor-buggy to stop it running backwards downhill and climbed a tree to reach a frightened kitten, the people of Jubilee Road wrote to the MAYOR. He signed a special certificate stating that Billy-William Bigheart was officially

THE KINDEST BOY IN THE UNIVERSE.

Mrs Bigheart had it framed in gold and it is hanging in their front hall.

Jim Jelly's Mum lost her job when the gym closed down and although she got another one eventually, she spent several months being at home all day. Mrs Bigheart took round a cake to cheer her up and Mrs Jelly thought that it was so delicious she asked how she could make one herself.

So Mrs Bigheart went once a week to give her cookery lessons and they became great friends.

When she got her new job, Mrs Jelly made sure she could leave work at three o'clock every afternoon, so that she could be home when Jim got in from school.

Sometimes, he brought Billy-William with him and they had cake his Mum had made, warm from the oven.

But Jim still goes round to the Bigheart's house a lot, especially during the school holidays and they still mooch about, looking for an adventure.

Every Saturday, they work at the Zoo, helping Reginald Crook with all the feeding and watering he has to do.

And making the baths full of banana custard.

And playing the game of wind-you-up-let-you-go with the straight snake.

Mr and Mrs Bigheart were given free passes to visit the zoo any time they like.

Last year, someone gave it six penguins, so the zoo built a pool for them, with a water chute but Jim Jelly was worried that they would get chilly in winter, so Mrs Bigheart started to knit jumpers for the penguins, helped by Jim's Mum. After that, they knitted jumpers and jackets and coats and trousers and bobble hats for all the animals, except the toothless crocodile, who just had his bath topped up with hot water from time to time.

There was even a rumour that Mr Bigheart was learning to knit.

But I don't know if that's true or not.